Royal Treasury

READ-AND-PLAY STORYBOOK

DISNEY PRESS

New York · Los Angeles

Contents

"Ariel's Dolphin Adventure" written by Lyra Spenser.
Illustrated by Studio IBOIX and Andrea Cagol.

"Rapunzel's Heroes" written by Barbara Bazaldua.
Illustrated by Denise Shimabukuro and Studio IBOIX.

"Aurora and the Helpful Dragon" written by Barbara Bazaldua.
Illustrated by Studio IBOIX and Gabriella Matta.

"Tiana and Her Loyal Friend" written by Natalie Amanda Leece.
Illustrated by Studio IBOIX and Walt Sturrock.
The movie *The Princess and the Frog* copyright © 2009 Disney,
story inspired in part by the book *The Frog Princess*
by E.D. Baker copyright © 2002, published by Bloomsbury Publishing, Inc.

For information address Disney Press,
1101 Flower Street, Glendale, California 91201.

Printed in the United States of America
First Edition
1 3 5 7 9 10 8 6 4 2
ILS V381-8386-5-14164
ISBN 978-1-4847-0434-9

Ariel's Dolphin Adventure

"Oh, Eric! This is wonderful!" Ariel said excitedly as she twirled around the ballroom with her prince. "I can dance with you *and* see the ocean!"

"Do you miss your sea friends?" he asked.

"Sometimes," Ariel replied a bit sadly. "But I love being with you."

Eric knew Ariel wished she could see her friends more. But he also knew that the rough water at the beach could be dangerous for them. That gave him an idea.

A few days later he brought Ariel to the lagoon. It now had a big wall to keep out dangerous sea creatures like sharks, but it also had a gate so that Ariel's friends could enter the lagoon. In fact, Flounder, Scuttle, and Sebastian were there to greet her!

"Oh, Eric!" Ariel gasped. "I love it!"

Ariel was so excited that she waded into the water. Then she stopped, seeing something else in the lagoon. "Look!" she exclaimed. As they watched, a baby dolphin leaped out of the water! "He's just a baby. I wonder where his mother is."

Flounder swam across the lagoon, but the baby dolphin raced away.

"Poor little guy," Flounder said. "He seems scared of me."

"We should find his mother right away!" Ariel said as she gently coaxed the baby to swim over to her.

"I bet she's on the other side of that wall. Don't worry, Ariel!" Flounder said. "We'll find her!"

But Sebastian and Flounder couldn't find the dolphin's mother. "Oh, Ariel! This is terrible," Sebastian said a few days later. "We have looked everywhere under the sea, but we cannot find her. King Triton will be so angry!"

Ariel was watching the little dolphin swim slowly around the lagoon. She knew that the confused baby was looking for his mother.

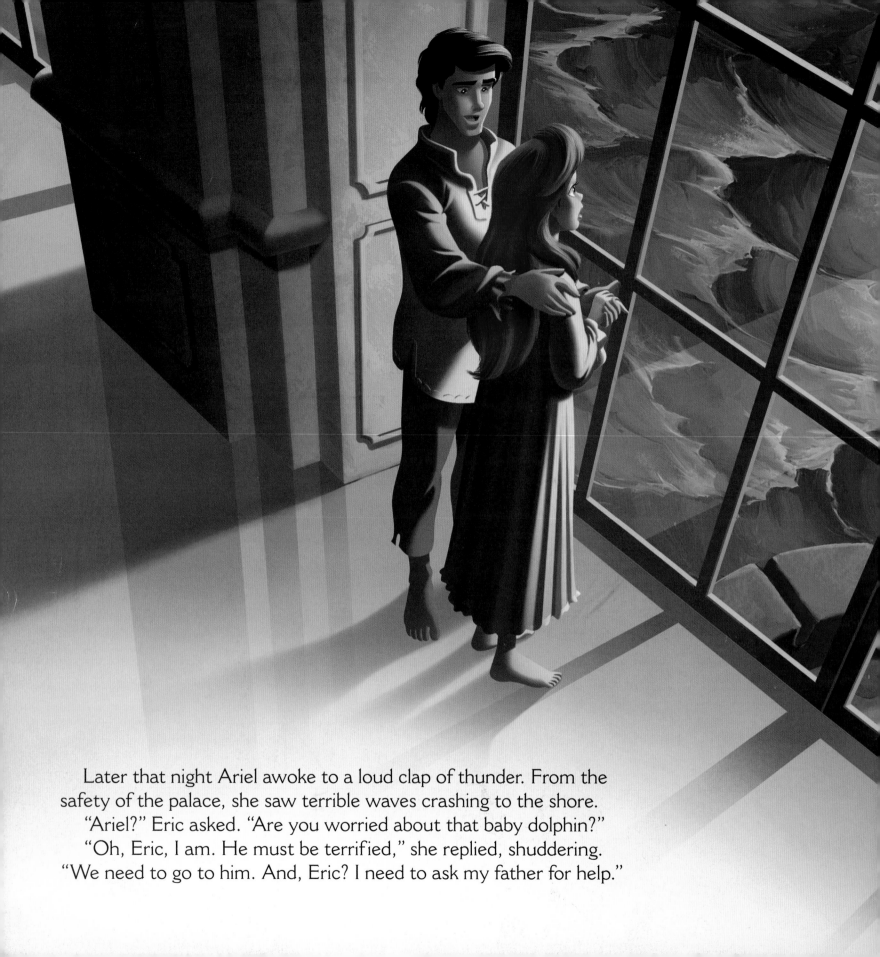

Later that night Ariel awoke to a loud clap of thunder. From the safety of the palace, she saw terrible waves crashing to the shore.

"Ariel?" Eric asked. "Are you worried about that baby dolphin?"

"Oh, Eric, I am. He must be terrified," she replied, shuddering. "We need to go to him. And, Eric? I need to ask my father for help."

Eric felt terrible. He now understood that he had made a
bad decision by closing in the lagoon. He followed Ariel into the
stormy night, ready to help in any way he could.

When they arrived at the lagoon, Flounder was trying to calm
the frightened baby dolphin.

"Go to him, Eric," Ariel said gently. "He feels safe with you."
Ariel looked into her prince's eyes, letting him know that she
trusted him with her sea friends.

Ariel carefully climbed onto the wall of the lagoon and called to all the sea creatures. "Help me, please!" she cried out. "I am Ariel, princess of the seas. I need my father, King Triton. Please help!"

Below the surface, sea creatures raced to find King Triton.

Eric tried to keep the baby dolphin safe from the crashing waves.
Holding him, Eric led him to the calmer waters near some rocks.
Suddenly there was a flash of light, and the storm calmed.
King Triton had arrived at the lagoon.

"What has happened here?" King Triton roared.

Eric looked down humbly. "It is entirely my fault, sir," he explained. "I built this wall to make a nice place for Ariel to visit her friends. I was wrong."

The king of the seas glared at Eric. Then, with a hint of a smile, he added, "Well, you *are* human, after all."

With a wave of his trident, King Triton called to all the dolphins and they quickly found the baby dolphin's mother! Frantically, she tried to get into the lagoon.

"Oh, dear!" Ariel exclaimed. "The gate won't open! She can't get in!"

Eric looked at King Triton. "Do you mind?"

"Not at all," the king replied. "Swim back, everyone!" He raised his trident and blasted down the wall.

That night, Eric and Ariel returned to the lagoon. It was filled with sea creatures.

"I love this place," Ariel said to her husband. "Thank you."

Just then the baby dolphin and his mother entered the lagoon, surfaced, and playfully splashed the prince and princess.

"I think that means we are forgiven!" Ariel laughed.

Rapunzel's Heroes

The day started nicely enough. It was the morning of my eighteenth birthday, and the birds were singing. Just yesterday, I'd taken a huge step—I had ventured out from the tall tower that had been my home all my life! And soon, if all went well, I'd be in the kingdom for the first time, watching the beautiful floating lights that were released there every year on the same date . . . my birthday.

It should have been a wonderful morning. But instead, here I was—me, Rapunzel—trying to rescue my guide from a horse!

I wasn't surprised that my guide had a problem
with a palace horse. I'd only known Flynn a short
while, but he had problems with almost everyone!
So, after I yanked Flynn free, I stepped in front
of the horse and stroked his nose. The name on
his chest plate read MAXIMUS.

Maximus thought Flynn was a thief (and all right, Flynn was a little misguided). Still, I hoped the horse wouldn't turn him over to the guards— at least, not until I could see the lights.

"Today is kind of the biggest day of my life," I explained. "It's also my birthday, just so you know."

Finally, Maximus stuck out his hoof . . . and Flynn shook it.

Together, we set off for the kingdom. Flynn thought we might travel faster if we rode on Maximus's back . . . but for some reason, Maximus did not agree.

Flynn tried again. He even managed to stay
on top of Maximus's head for a few seconds.
Then Maximus lowered his head, and
Flynn tumbled into the mud again.

"I don't like this horse!"
Flynn howled. "And this
horse doesn't like *me*!"

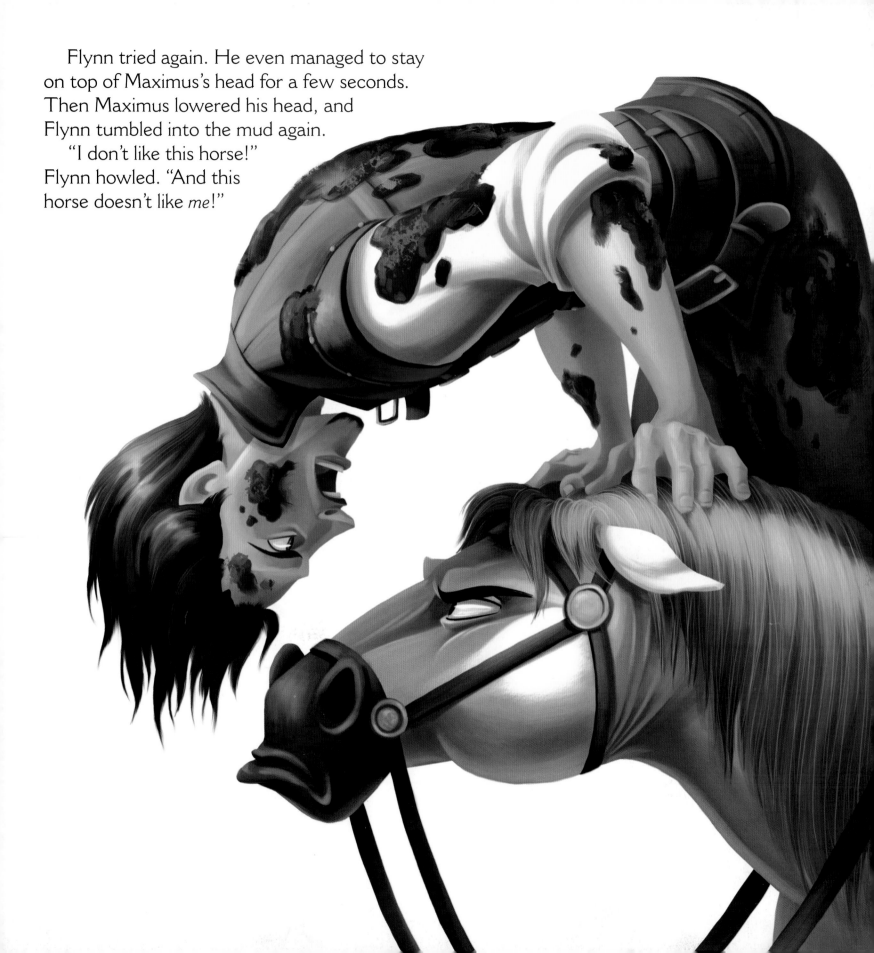

Finally, Flynn decided we'd travel faster if we just started walking.

"Do you have this problem with all horses?" I asked.

"No," Flynn replied. "When I was growing up in the orphanage, I dreamed of becoming a swashbuckling hero—and swashbuckling heroes love horses. No, it's *this* horse. *He's* the problem!"

As we walked, Maximus flicked his tail in Flynn's face. So Flynn poked Maximus in the ribs. Then Maximus stepped on Flynn's foot . . . and Flynn yanked on Maximus's bridle.

I sighed. Those two just had to get along, or my special day would be ruined. Luckily, I had an idea. "I know!" I told Flynn. "I'll *teach* you how to get along with Maximus!"

Flynn grumbled but watched as I stroked Maximus under his chin. Then I scratched his ears. Pascal, who was sitting on Maximus's head, helped.

"See?" I said, nuzzling Maximus's face. "Now you do it."

"*Ugh!* No way!" Flynn protested.
"That's just plain—"
"NOW!" I commanded.
I don't think it was *too* hard on them.

Getting into the kingdom was a little tricky, because Flynn was wanted by the palace guards. Maximus and Flynn managed it, though, by working together. Those two were making good progress!

I think Maximus was a little surprised as he watched Flynn that day.

Maybe he realized Flynn wasn't so bad after all. . . .

37

Maximus still wouldn't let Flynn climb onto his back, though.

That evening, when it was time to see the
lanterns being released, Flynn surprised me by
taking me out in a boat. He said that watching
from the water would give us the best view.

There was another surprise, too. Flynn gave a bag
of apples to Maximus! The horse looked suspicious.

"What? I bought them," Flynn responded.

Maximus whinnied happily as Flynn paddled away.

"Most of them," Flynn muttered under his breath.

We didn't expect to be gone long. Maximus waited and waited. Finally, a boat bumped up against the dock. But it was a different boat, and it was carrying only Flynn—who was tied to the mast with a stolen crown on his lap! He seemed confused, and was yelling, "Rapunzel? Rapunzel!"

Maximus backed out of sight as the palace guards came forward and arrested Flynn. Maximus didn't know where I was, but he knew that something had gone very, very wrong.

Maximus raced away, but he wasn't leaving Flynn. He was going for help!

With a lot of hoof stomping and loud snorting, Maximus convinced our friends at the Snuggly Duckling tavern to follow him back to the castle.

Waving their clubs and axes, they raced to the kingdom, broke
into the prison, and freed Flynn.
Of course, getting him *out* of the prison was another problem . . .

. . . but Maximus was ready and waiting!

Together, Max and Flynn galloped through the streets, leaped over guards, and dashed through the town's gates just as they were closing.

Flynn could hardly believe he was riding Max. Suddenly, he realized he trusted the horse. They were a team.

I won't explain everything that happened that day, but my life did change forever. Mother Gothel, who had imprisoned me, showed her evil side. Then I learned my true identity. I was a princess and had been stolen from my parents long ago!

But Flynn fought for me. To save me, he had to cut my long golden hair, but that didn't matter to me—or to him. He loved me for myself.
It was quite a day.

Afterward, we could have ridden back to the kingdom, but Flynn wouldn't allow it. Instead, we *walked*!

"He ran all night," Flynn explained, as he patted Maximus. "He's tired and needs a rest." Flynn paused. "You know, I felt like a real hero today." Then he turned to Max. "But you are an even bigger hero. If it weren't for you, Rapunzel and I wouldn't be here."

Flynn and Max were both heroes. But just as important, they were friends.

Aurora and the Helpful Dragon

"I'll race you to the lookout point!" Princess Aurora called to Prince Phillip as they galloped through the forest one sunny fall morning. She sped away on her horse, Moonlight, with Prince Phillip close behind.

Just as Aurora and Phillip rounded a bend, they heard a funny noise. A small dragon popped from behind a tree and scampered toward Aurora.

"Oh, he's so cute!" Aurora exclaimed as she dismounted.

"Grrgrrgrr?" the little dragon murmured, clambering into Aurora's lap. But Phillip wanted to protect his wife. "Dragons can be dangerous!" The little dragon shook his head, no.

"I think he's saying he's not dangerous," Aurora laughed. "Please, let's take him home. I'm going to name him Crackle!"

"He *does* seem like a harmless little fellow," Phillip agreed.

But Moonlight was still afraid. She tossed her mane and pawed the ground. Crackle's tail drooped sadly. Then he grinned his funny little grin. Suddenly, he licked Moonlight's nose with his long, warm tongue. Moonlight blinked with surprise and nuzzled Crackle under the chin. The little dragon giggled.

"Moonlight likes Crackle!" Aurora laughed.

When Phillip and Aurora rode into the courtyard, the three fairies were hanging banners for King Stefan and the Queen, who were coming for a ball that night.

"Come, my dear, let's practice dancing!" Phillip said to his princess.

Flora gasped when she saw Crackle. "Dragons can be dangerous."

"Remember the last one!" Fauna added.

"Oooh, I think he's sweet," Merryweather spoke up.

"Grrrgrr," Crackle babbled.

"He thinks you're sweet, too," Aurora told Merryweather as Prince Phillip swept his princess across the courtyard.

Just then, Crackle noticed a kitten in Fauna's workbasket.

Crackle listened to the cute kitten purring. Crackle scrunched up his mouth and closed his eyes.

"Purrgrr, purrgrr!" Crackle tried to purr. Clouds of smoke puffed from his nose and mouth.

"*Aachoo! Aachooooie! Ah-ah-ah-CHOO!*" The fairies sneezed so hard that they fluttered backward.

"Please–*achoo*–stop trying to purr!" Fauna exclaimed.

Crackle looked sad for a moment. Then he saw the kitten playing with a ball of yarn from the workbasket, and his eyes lit up. He snatched a ball of yarn with his mouth. *Whoosh!*—it caught fire. Merryweather put the fire out with her wand.

"Oh, Crackle," Aurora said gently. "You're not a kitten. You're a dragon." Crackle's lower lip trembled.

Just then, Crackle saw Phillip leading the horses into the stables. A dog followed Phillip, barking and wagging its tail. Crackle wagged his tail and ran to the stables, too.

"Woofgrr, woofgrr," he tried to bark. Flames shot from his mouth and caught some straw on fire. Phillip poured water on the burning straw.

"You're not a dog," he said kindly, shooing Crackle away.

When Aurora saw Crackle creep from the stable, she carried him into the castle and cuddled him on a window seat. A bird was singing outside. Crackle's ears perked up and his eyes shone hopefully.

"LAAAlaagrr!" he bellowed.

King Hubert heard the racket and rushed into the room.

"Oh, my, my, my! How did a dragon get in here?" he blustered.

Frightened by the king, Crackle jumped from the window seat and ran into the garden. Aurora ran after him. At last she found the little dragon sitting beside a waterfall that splashed down from one pool to another. Crackle was studying a fish swimming in the lowest pool.

Before Aurora could stop him, Crackle splashed into the water. The startled fish leaped into a higher pool.

"Crackle, you're not a fish!" Aurora exclaimed as she pulled Crackle from
the pool. "You're not a kitten, or a dog, or a bird either. You're a dragon!"
Tears rolled down Crackle's face. "Grrgrrgrr," he sobbed.
Suddenly, Aurora understood.
"Do you think no one will like you because you're a dragon?" she asked.
Crackle nodded and whimpered sadly.

"Crackle, you can't change being a dragon," Aurora said kindly. "But you don't have to be a dangerous dragon. You can be a brave, helpful dragon."

Crackle stopped crying. "Grrgrrgrrgrr?" he growled hopefully.

Before Aurora could answer, thunder boomed. Wind blew black clouds over the sun. Aurora snatched up Crackle. She reached the castle doors just as the rain began to pour down.

Everyone was gathered in the grand hallway, watching the storm.

"I'm afraid King Stefan and the Queen might lose their way on the road above the cliffs," Prince Phillip said, his voice filled with concern. "I should ride out to help."

Aurora looked at Crackle. "Do you want to show everyone that you're a brave and helpful dragon?" she asked.

"GRRRgrrrgrr!" Crackle exclaimed enthusiastically.

"Fly to the top of the highest castle tower," Aurora explained. "Then blow the largest, brightest flames you can."

Aurora watched him as the little fellow soared upward.

"Come on, everyone!" the princess called. She ran to get a better view of the watchtower, with Phillip and the others following closely behind.

Everyone tried to see Crackle at the top of the tower, but the storm was too dark and strong. Suddenly, they saw huge flames. They were coming from little Crackle! Gold and red light flashed in the sky above the watchtower.

Again and again, Crackle blew his flames until, at last, Phillip shouted, "I see King Stefan and the Queen! They're almost here!"

Everyone hurried to greet the visiting royals.

"The tower light saved us!" King Stefan exclaimed. "I need one like it!"

At that moment Crackle flew happily to join in the fun.

"Well, there he is! Our new tower light," King Hubert said with a laugh.

"A dragon?" King Stefan asked. "But dragons are danger—"

"Not Crackle," Aurora interrupted. "He's a brave and helpful dragon!"

That night at the ball, Crackle lit the candles, warmed food, and kept the fireplace blazing. King Hubert and the fairies were so pleased that they took turns scratching Crackle beneath his chin.

As Prince Phillip and Aurora danced, Crackle trotted beside them. Outside, it was cold and stormy. But inside, everyone was happy and warm—especially Crackle the helpful dragon.

Tiana and
Her Loyal Friend

It was a balmy afternoon in New Orleans. Big Daddy was in the mood for some good food and good times with friends.

"Charlotte, honey!" he called out to his daughter. "How about going to Tiana's Palace for supper tonight—"

"Oh, Daddy, that would be wonderful! Just give me a minute to change."

Later, as they drove off, nobody noticed Stella the hound asleep in the back of the car!

But Stella didn't mind. In fact, the one thing that woke her up was the smell of Tiana's beignets when they reached the restaurant. Stella loved Tiana's beignets, so the hound followed her nose right into the restaurant's back kitchen.

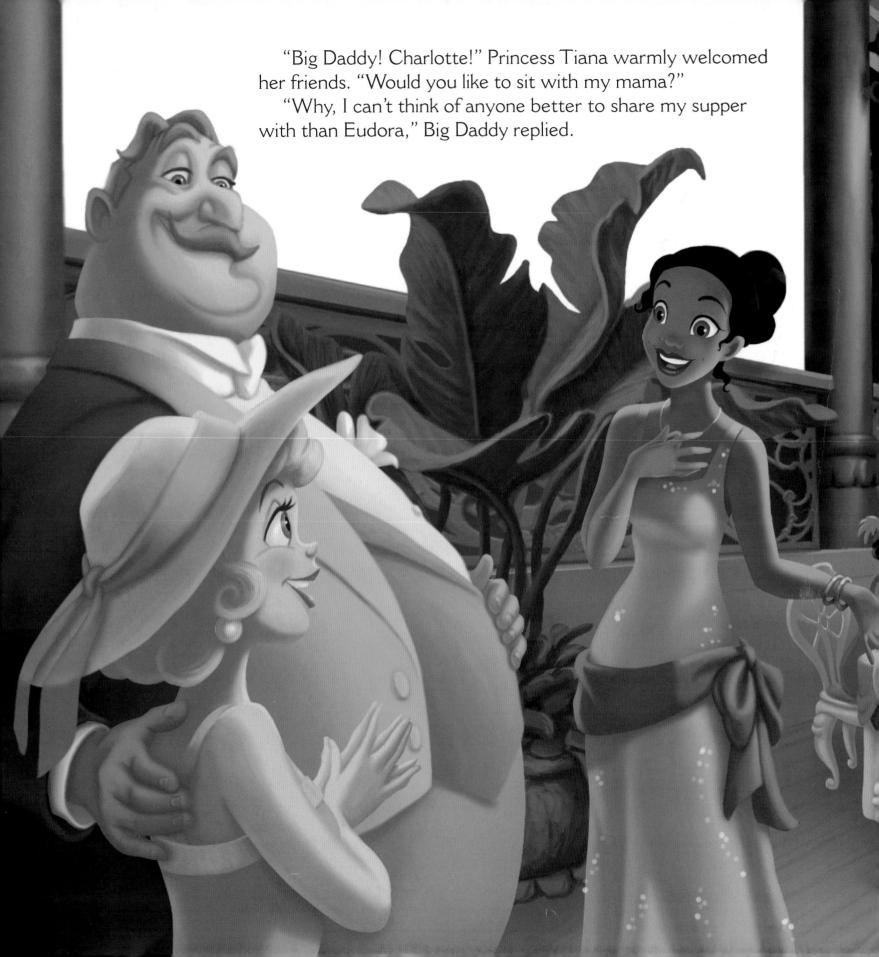

"Big Daddy! Charlotte!" Princess Tiana warmly welcomed her friends. "Would you like to sit with my mama?"

"Why, I can't think of anyone better to share my supper with than Eudora," Big Daddy replied.

Meanwhile, Stella smelled nothing but goodness in the kitchen.
"Lookee here!" shouted one of the cooks. "We have a visitor!
Here you go, puppy—have some of this gumbo. It's a new recipe!"

Stella spent a happy evening in the kitchen getting well
fed and petted, while Charlotte and Big Daddy dined to
Louis's jazz music and good conversation with their friends.

81

After the last jazz number was played, Prince Naveen's parents, the king and queen of Maldonia, got up to leave, offering Eudora a ride home.

"Why, thank you," Eudora said. Turning to Princess Tiana, she added, "I have never heard the band play quite so well as tonight. And that new gumbo—absolutely delicious. I'll see you later, sweetheart."

As everyone said their good-byes, still nobody knew about Stella . . .

. . . not until Louis entered the kitchen for his evening meal with the rest of the band.

"Grrr! Woof!" Stella was terrified of the giant alligator.

"Oh, now hold on, little dog!" Louis spoke to Stella. "I'm not here to eat you. I just wanted a taste of the chef's new gumbo!"

The kitchen staff backed away. They just heard growls coming from the dog and the gator.

Princess Tiana and Prince Naveen also heard the commotion as they re-entered the restaurant after bidding their friends and family good night.

As soon as the prince and princess entered the kitchen, they saw a very frightened Stella plastered against a wall, barking at Louis.

"What is going on with you two?" Princess Tiana said, concerned for Stella.

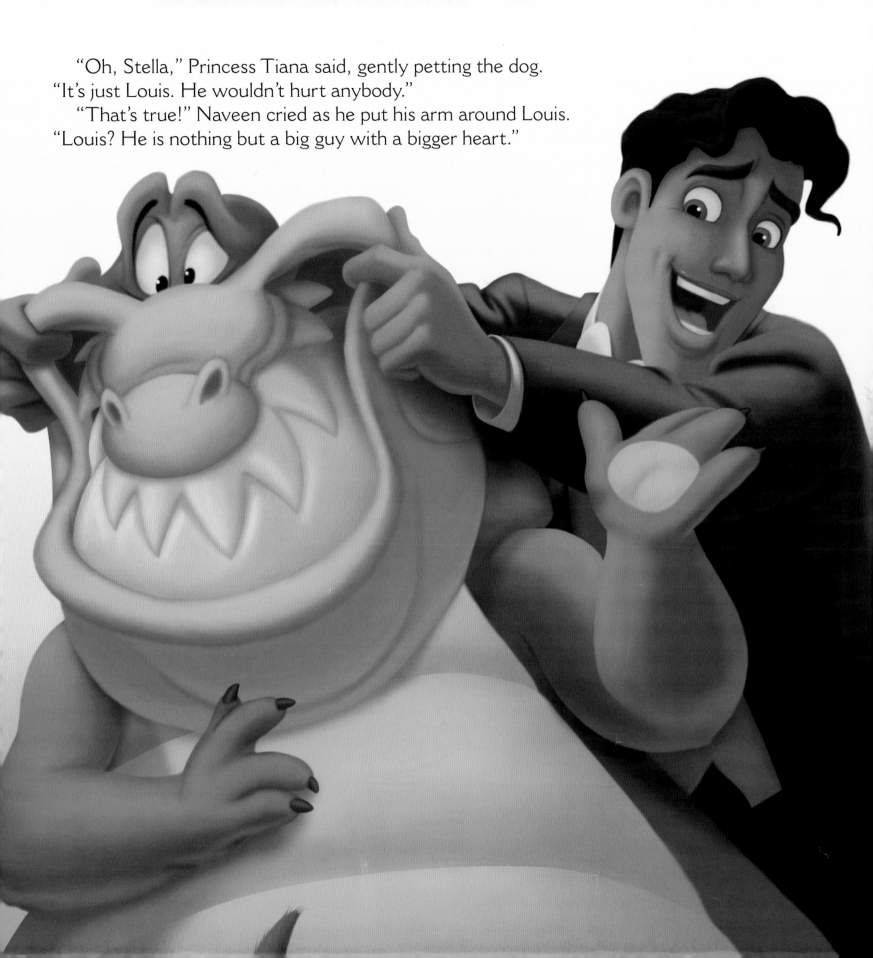

"Oh, Stella," Princess Tiana said, gently petting the dog.
"It's just Louis. He wouldn't hurt anybody."

"That's true!" Naveen cried as he put his arm around Louis.
"Louis? He is nothing but a big guy with a bigger heart."

"Go ahead, Stella," Princess Tiana encouraged the dog. "Naveen will hold on to Louis, and you just walk right over to them."

Cautiously, Stella walked toward Louis, with Tiana by her side. Stella sniffed Louis and then turned back toward the food. Tiana giggled. Naveen giggled. Louis wanted to giggle, but he thought he might scare Stella all over again.

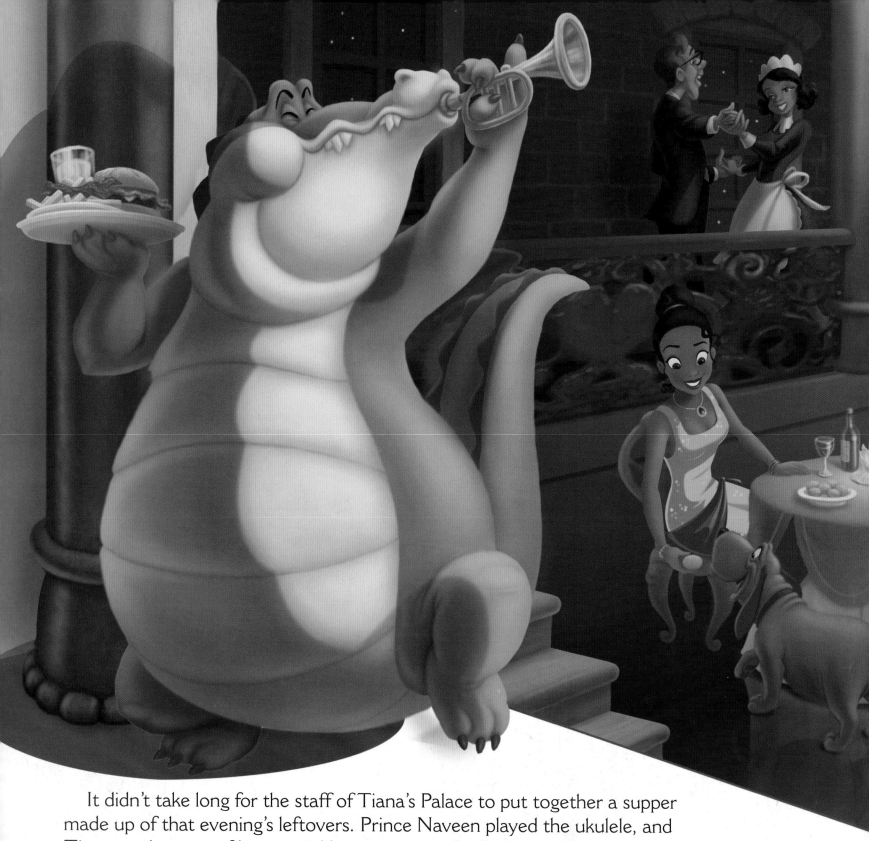

It didn't take long for the staff of Tiana's Palace to put together a supper made up of that evening's leftovers. Prince Naveen played the ukulele, and Tiana made some of her special beignets—just for Stella.

Princess Tiana had to smile. These were truly the good times her father had imagined having at their restaurant.

Before dawn, the prince and princess dropped Stella off at the LaBouff estate. No one had even noticed she was missing yet!

"Good night, Stella," Princess Tiana said, giving the dog a big hug. "And don't be a stranger. When I stop by, I expect you to come out and get your own beignets."

Stella gave one last woof and went toward the house. She had had the best night of her life.